HEINEMANN GUI[illegible]

INTERMEDIA[illegible]

BRAM STOKER

Dracula

Retold by Margaret Tarner

HEINEMANN

HEINEMANN GUIDED READERS

INTERMEDIATE LEVEL

Series Editor: John Milne

The Heinemann Guided Readers provide a choice of enjoyable reading material for learners of English. The series is published at five levels – Starter, Beginner, Elementary, Intermediate and Upper. At **Intermediate Level**, the control of content and language has the following main features:

Information Control

Information which is vital to the understanding of the story is presented in an easily assimilated manner and is repeated when necessary. Difficult allusion and metaphor are avoided and cultural backgrounds are made explicit.

Structure Control

Most of the structures used in the Readers will be familiar to students who have completed an elementary course of English. Other grammatical features may occur, but their use is made clear through context and reinforcement. This ensures that the reading, as well as being enjoyable, provides a continual learning situation for the students. Sentences are limited in most cases to a maximum of three clauses and within sentences there is a balanced use of adverbial and adjectival phrases. Great care is taken with pronoun reference.

Vocabulary Control

There is a basic vocabulary of approximately 1,600 words. Help is given to the students in the form of illustrations, which are closely related to the text.

Glossary

Some difficult words and phrases in this book are important for understanding the story. Some of these words are explained in the story, some are shown in the pictures, and others are marked with a number like this . . .[3] Words with a number are explained in the Glossary on page 59.

Contents

Introductory Notes

Prince Dracula

The story of Dracula was written in 1897. The author, Bram Stoker, had read about a prince called Dracula. Dracula was the ruler of a country called Transylvania in the fifteenth century. Transylvania is not marked on maps today. It is now part of Romania.

Prince Dracula was a very cruel man. He killed many people in horrible ways. One way was to throw them onto the sharp points of stakes fixed in the ground.

Many stories were told about Prince Dracula. The stories were about his cruelty to the people he killed. After his death, Dracula's grave was opened. But his body was not found in the grave. The people of Transylvania believed that Dracula was not dead.

Vampires

At the time of this story, people in Transylvania believed in vampires. They believed that vampires did not die. Vampires rested during the day and moved about at night. They attacked people and drank their blood. The people who were attacked also became vampires. They did not die. They attacked other people and drank their blood. So more and more vampires came into the world.

The people in Transylvania were very frightened of vampires. They believed many strange things about vampires. They said that vampires could climb up and down high walls and fly through the air. Vampires were able to change into birds or animals. They could become dust or thick mist. Vampires knew what people were thinking. They could make people do what they wanted.

Transylvanians protected themselves against vampires in

many ways. They wore a Christian cross around their necks. They put garlic plants in their houses. They believed that praying to God would protect them from vampires. And they believed that vampires were turned away by pieces of holy bread. This is bread which is blessed by the priest in a Christian church.

Three things had to be done to destroy vampires. First, you had to find the place where the vampires rested during the day. Then you had to put sharp, wooden stakes through the vampires' hearts. Finally, you had to cut off their heads.

"Dracula" is a horror story. People like to be frightened by horror stories. This is one of the most famous horror stories ever written. Do not read this book late at night when you are alone!

1

The Road to Castle Dracula

My name is Jonathan Harker. I am a lawyer and I live in London. About seven years ago, some strange and terrible things happened to me. Many of my dear friends were in danger too. At last we have decided to tell the story of that terrible time.

Part of my work is to find houses in England for rich people who live in foreign countries. At the beginning of 1875, I received a letter from Transylvania, a country in Eastern Europe. The letter was from a rich man called Count Dracula. He wanted to buy a house near London.

The Count asked me to find him an old house with a large garden. The price of the house was not important. I found him a large, old house to the east of London. I wrote to the Count and he agreed to buy it. There were many papers which he had to sign[1]. To my surprise, Count Dracula invited me to visit him in his castle in Transylvania. 'Bring the papers with you,' he wrote in his letter. 'I can sign them here.'

I was very busy and did not want to go. Transylvania was far away and few English people had been there. There was another reason too. I was going to get married in the autumn to my darling Mina. I did not want to leave England until we were married.

But Mina said that I should go.

'The Count is a rich man,' she said. 'You may be able to do more business with him. You can travel most of the way by train. In two weeks, you will be home again.'

So I accepted Count Dracula's invitation. I left England at the end of April. Mina gave me a book about Transylvania to read on the train.

On the morning of 4th May, I reached Bistritz, a small town in Transylvania. It was a beautiful day. The sun was shining on the great Carpathian Mountains. Somewhere, high up in those mountains, was Castle Dracula where the Count lived. The coach[2] from Bistritz would take me to the Borgo Pass. There, the Count's carriage would meet me. The coach left from the inn[3] in Bistritz at three o'clock.

I had six hours to wait. I decided to have a meal. Nobody in the inn spoke English, but the innkeeper spoke some German. He welcomed me and I was soon eating a good meal.

The inn was very crowded. I watched all the people in their brightly-coloured clothes. They were speaking in languages I could not understand. I drank some more wine and called to the innkeeper.

'What can you tell me about Count Dracula?' I asked him. 'Have you ever seen his castle?'

The innkeeper walked away without answering my questions. All the people in the inn stopped talking. They looked at me in fear and surprise. Then they all began to talk at the same time. I heard the name 'Dracula' and another word, repeated several times.

I looked at my dictionary. They were saying the word 'vampire'[4]. Where had I read the word before? I opened the book that Mina had given me.

There are many old stories about the vampires of Transylvania, I read. Vampires are men and women who never die. Vampires have long, sharp teeth. They bite the throats of living people. Then they drink their blood. Everyone in Transylvania fears vampires. People often wear a cross[5] to keep themselves safe . . .

I shut the book quickly. Did people believe these stories?

It was time for me to leave. I paid for my meal. Then I walked outside and got into the coach. There was a crowd of people outside the inn. Suddenly the innkeeper ran forward and spoke to me through the coach window.

'Must you go to Castle Dracula?' he said. 'Do not go to that terrible place!'

'I have important business with the Count,' I answered.

'Then take this,' the innkeeper said, 'and may God help you!' And he put a gold cross on a chain into my hand.

As the coach began to move, strange thoughts went through my mind. Who was this man I was going to meet? Did Count Dracula have strange powers? I could not believe it.

The coach began to move more quickly. The sun shone on the trees and the water of little rivers. There was snow on the tops of the highest mountains. What a beautiful country Transylvania was!

The mountains were closer to us now, and the road went higher and higher. Shadows grew longer as the sun began to go down behind the mountains. Then suddenly, the light had gone. The mountains and sky were dark. The coach went faster and faster. I could hear a terrible sound. It was the howling of wolves[6].

The moon was shining now. I could see dark shapes near the road. The coach went higher and higher. And now I could see a narrow road to the right. The coach stopped. We were at the Borgo Pass.

Down the narrow road came a small carriage, pulled by four black horses. As the carriage stopped, its driver shouted, 'I have come from Castle Dracula! Where is the Englishman?'

'Here!' I replied. The driver jumped down from the carriage. He took my bag and held me by the arm. In a moment, I was sitting beside him and the black horses were galloping up the narrow road.

The driver wore a black cloak[7] and his hat was pulled down over his face. The mountains were high black walls on both sides of us. We were going so fast that I had to hold onto the carriage with both hands. Black clouds covered the moon. The carriage had no lights and I could see nothing. Wolves howled all around us. The driver laughed. As the horses went faster, I closed my eyes in fear.

Down the narrow road came a small carriage, pulled by four black horses.

Then suddenly, the journey was over. The driver pulled me down from the carriage. He threw my bag beside me. In a moment, the carriage and the driver had disappeared. I had arrived at Castle Dracula!

2

A Prisoner in the Castle

I looked up at the high castle walls. There were no lights in any of the windows. In front of me was a great wooden door.

As I stood there, I heard the door being unlocked. It opened slowly. A very tall old man was standing there. He held a lamp in his hand. His hair and face were white and he was dressed in black. He held his lamp up high and said, 'Welcome to my home. Enter Castle Dracula, Mr Harker.'

As I stepped inside, Count Dracula took hold of my arm. He was terribly strong and his hand was as cold as ice. The Count locked the door carefully and put the keys into his pocket.

I followed him down long passages and up winding[8] stairs. I walked like a man in a dream. At last, the Count opened a door and led me into a room without windows. I could see two open doors. Through one door, I could see a bedroom. Through the other door, I could see food and drink on a table.

'When you are ready, my dear friend,' the Count said, 'I shall be waiting for you.'

In a few minutes, I was sitting at the table. I was very hungry. The Count told me he had already eaten.

Later, we sat together near the fire. The Count spoke good English and he asked me many questions. I was tired and I began

'Welcome to my home. Enter Castle Dracula, Mr Harker.'

to feel very ill. The castle was completely silent. But outside the wolves were howling.

'Can you hear the children of the night?' the Count said quietly. 'Listen to their music!'

Count Dracula's face was very close to mine. The fire made his eyes shine with a red light. There was an unpleasant smell in the room. I wondered what it was. The Count smiled. He had very red lips and his teeth were long and sharp.

'You are tired,' he said. 'It is time for you to sleep.'

That night, I had strange and terrible dreams. In my dreams, I heard the sound of wolves and strange laughter.

When I woke up, it was late in the morning. There was fresh food in the other room and a note from the Count on the table.

I have to leave you alone today, I read. *You can go anywhere in the Castle. But some doors are locked. Do not try to open them. D.*

I saw no one all day. But I found the Count's library. It was full of books about England and I spent the day reading them. I was still reading when Count Dracula returned in the evening.

'These books are my good friends,' he said. 'They have taught me a lot about your country. And now I have you, Mr Harker, to talk to.'

'You speak English well, Count,' I said. The Count smiled and showed his sharp, white teeth.

'You must tell me about my new house,' he said. 'And you have papers for me to sign.'

I showed Count Dracula the maps and photographs I had brought with me.

'The house is about 22 kilometres to the east of London,' I told him. 'It is large and parts of it are very old.'

'Good,' said the Count. 'I have always lived in an old house. I could not live in a new one.'

'The gardens have a high wall around them,' I went on. 'This is a photograph of the chapel[9]. It is the oldest part of the house.'

'So I shall be near the tombs[10] of the dead,' said Count

Dracula quietly. He held the photograph in his hand. For the first time, I noticed his long, pointed nails.

The Count went on talking all night long. Once, I must have fallen asleep. I sat up suddenly. Count Dracula was leaning[11] over me. His breath had a terrible smell. What did it remind me of? As I opened my eyes he turned away.

'Well, my friend,' said Dracula, 'We have been talking all night. You are tired. Go to bed and sleep.'

But I did not sleep well. My mind was troubled. Once more, I had terrible dreams.

It was very early when I woke up. I decided to dress and shave[12].

I looked round my bedroom. To my surprise, there was no mirror. Fortunately, I had brought a small shaving mirror with me. I hung it by the window and began to shave.

'Good morning, my friend,' said a voice behind me. I was so surprised that my razor slipped and I cut myself. I turned. There

stood Count Dracula! He had come up behind me. Why had I not seen his face in my mirror?

The Count saw the blood on my face. He made a strange sound and his hands moved towards my throat. His eyes shone with red fire. Then his hands touched the cross around my neck and the fire in his eyes disappeared.

'Take care,' he said. 'It is dangerous to cut yourself in Castle Dracula. And this mirror is not needed here.'

As he spoke, he threw my mirror out of the open window. It broke on the stones far below. The Count turned and left the room. When I went to have my breakfast, he had gone. I was by myself once again.

I was very restless. I spent the day looking round the castle. Wherever I went, I found locked doors. Some windows opened but they were high up in the castle walls. The ground was hundreds of metres below.

There was no way out of the castle. Except for Count Dracula, I was completely alone. Was I a prisoner in this strange and terrible place?

3

The Vampires

Time passed slowly. I always saw the Count at night. During the day, I sat in the library, reading a book. Sometimes I walked slowly through the long passages of the castle.

The papers were signed and I was ready to leave. But Count Dracula would not let me go. Every evening, he asked me more questions about England. Every evening, I asked to leave. But he always smiled and would not answer.

I was full of fear. The Count had a strange power over me which grew stronger every day. I could not think clearly. Would I ever escape from Castle Dracula?

Then one day, I found a room with an unlocked door. As soon as I went into the room, I felt very tired. I lay down on a couch[13] opposite the window.

When I opened my eyes, it was getting dark. But the air was full of golden dust. It slowly changed into the shapes of three young women. They were very beautiful. I felt afraid of them and yet I wanted them to touch me. I wanted them to kiss me with their soft, red lips. My body felt heavy. I could not move.

'Go on,' one woman said to another, 'you are the first. But he is young and strong. There will be kisses for us all!'

One of the women moved towards me. She smiled. Her teeth were sharp and white. I closed my eyes as she leant over me. I felt her long hair on my face. She made a strange sound and licked her

red lips. Her sharp teeth touched my throat. Now, I thought, now, now! Kiss me, kiss me!

There was a sudden shout. Count Dracula had come into the room and pulled the woman away from me.

'Get back, he is mine. How dare you touch him!' he cried.

'Oh, you are cruel,' said the woman, with a terrible laugh. 'Have you never been in love?'

'You know I have,' the Count replied. 'That is why you are here. Wait a little longer, you will have your chance!'

I must have fainted[14]. When I woke again, I was in my own room. It was daylight. The sun was shining brightly. I could see the gold cross on the table, where I had left it.

It was now 19th May. I stayed near my room all day. When I saw the Count in the evening, it was difficult to hide my fear. But he smiled as usual and said, 'My dear Mr Harker, I am happy to have you as my guest. But I know you want to see your Mina again.'

The Count put some paper and three envelopes on the table.

'The post in Transylvania is not good,' he said. 'But write what I tell you and Mina will get your letters.'

He told me what to write. He made me put dates on the letters. The last letter was dated 29th June. What could I do? I was terribly afraid. I wrote down the Count's words. In the last letter, I told Mina that I had left the castle and was on my way home.

I knew then that Count Dracula meant to kill me. But not yet. It was six weeks until 29th June. I had six more weeks to live!

The days went by. I was Dracula's prisoner and he . . . what was he? Would I ever know the truth about him?

Then it was 29th June. That night, Count Dracula spoke to me.

'My dear friend, you and I must part. Tomorrow I must go to England. Perhaps one day we shall meet again.'

What did he mean? I had to find out the truth. I decided to follow Dracula to his room. He went in and locked the door behind him. I heard a window open.

I looked out of a window in the passage. I could see the window of the Count's room. As I watched, Dracula came out of the window and moved down the wall – head first! His black cloak looked like the wings of a huge bird. In the bright moonlight, I watched him move down the wall and out of sight!

I had to think. I had to make a plan. I went back to my room and looked again at my book about Transylvania. Vampires always hunted and killed at night. Sometimes they became animals. But during the day, vampires lost their strange powers.

I had never seen Count Dracula during the day. If I went to his room in daylight, perhaps he could not harm me. Perhaps I could take his keys and escape at last.

All night, I waited by the window in the passage. At dawn[15], Count Dracula returned. When the sun was high in the sky, I climbed out of the window. I moved carefully down the wall and across to the Count's open window.

There was nothing in the room except a great heap of golden coins. One door was locked. But the second one opened and I went through it. A stone stairway went down and down to a long passage. I was in an old chapel. The stones in the floor had been taken away. There were great holes where the earth had been.

The chapel was full of wooden boxes – fifty of them. Their lids had not been fixed on. Each box was full of earth.

One box was covered and I lifted the lid. There, on a heap of earth, lay Count Dracula!

His white hair was now dark grey. His thin, white face was fat and red. Fresh blood ran from his lips and there was a terrible

smell, the smell of blood! The Vampire was resting after his meal. His eyes were open, but he did not move. I could see his long, white teeth.

At that moment, I heard shouts and the sound of many feet. I ran back through the door and into the passage. The door closed behind me. I stood there, listening.

The chapel was full of men. They were hammering[16] down the lids of the boxes. Then I heard them pulling the boxes along the ground. A door was shut and locked. Count Dracula was on his way to England and I was locked inside his castle! I ran down the passage, up the stone stairs and back to the Count's room. I put some of the gold coins in my pockets and ran to the open window. The ground was many metres below. With a prayer to God, I climbed out of the window and moved slowly down the wall . . .

4

A Visit to Hythe

In England, Mina was waiting for Jonathan Harker to return. His letters to her from Castle Dracula had been short and strange. Mina was worried. Was Jonathan ill? Why did he not return to England.

In the middle of July, Mina was invited to stay with her friend, Lucy West. Lucy and her husband, Arthur, lived in the little town of Hythe, by the sea. Arthur West was a doctor.

'Arthur is in Amsterdam,' Lucy wrote. 'He is staying with Professor Van Helsing, his old teacher. Come and stay with me until your Jonathan returns. Hythe is not far from London. The sea air will be good for you.'

Mina travelled down to Hythe the following day. The weather was good and the two young women went out walking every day. Sometimes, they walked by the sea. But most of all Lucy liked to walk to the old church on the hill. She enjoyed sitting in the quiet old churchyard[17].

Mina and Lucy slept in the same bedroom. One night, near the end of July, Mina woke up suddenly. Lucy was walking out of the bedroom door, but she was fast asleep. Mina took her friend back to bed. Lucy did not wake up and, in the morning, she remembered nothing.

On 8th August, the weather changed. Black clouds covered the sky. The air felt heavy and there was a thick mist over the sea. The storm came soon after midnight. Lucy was very excited[18] by the thunder and lightning. She sat by the window all night, looking at the sea.

By morning, everything was quiet. But there was a mist over the sea. Lucy's servant told the two friends that a ship had been wrecked on the shore[19].

'Was it an English ship? Are the poor sailors safe?' Lucy asked her.

'It was a Russian ship,' the woman replied. 'It had come from a place called Varna. There was something very strange about the ship. There was no one on it, living or dead!

'But as soon as the ship touched the shore,' the woman went on, 'a huge dog jumped down. It ran away up the hill. There was another strange thing, too. The ship was full of big wooden boxes. Some men came from London and took them away. When the boxes were taken off the ship one of them broke open. It was full of earth! Who would bring earth all that way? I cannot understand it.'

Lucy's face had gone white, but her eyes were shining.

'Let's walk up to the church, Mina,' she said. 'Perhaps we shall find the dog.' But the churchyard was empty and no one had seen the animal.

That night, Mina heard a noise and woke up. Lucy's bed was empty and the bedroom door was wide open! Lucy was nowhere in the house. Mina put on her clothes and her shoes. Then, taking shoes and a shawl[20] for Lucy, Mina ran out into the silent street.

Where had Lucy gone? Mina looked up and down the empty street. Was Lucy in the churchyard? Mina ran up the hill and stopped for a moment at the churchyard gate.

Yes, there was Lucy! Was there something moving behind her? Mina thought she saw a white face and two red eyes. But when she reached Lucy, her friend was alone.

Lucy was half asleep. Mina put the shawl round her friend and took her back to the house. When Mina was putting her to bed she saw two red marks on Lucy's throat. Mina wondered what had made the marks. But she said nothing to Lucy.

From that time, Lucy became paler and paler. Her pretty face grew

Mina thought she saw a white face and two red eyes.

thin and white. Mina knew her friend was ill. She wanted to send Arthur a telegram[21], but Lucy would not let her.

'Arthur is doing some important work in Professor Van Helsing's hospital,' Lucy said. 'I do not want to worry him.'

But every night, Lucy left her bed while she was asleep. Mina had to lock the bedroom door to keep her friend safe.

One night, Mina found Lucy leaning out of the open window. A huge, black bird was sitting beside her. When Mina moved near, the bird flew slowly away. Lucy was fast asleep but she was holding her throat. The two marks were still there. They looked very red and painful.

Then on 19th August, Mina received a letter from a hospital in Budapest.

'Oh, Lucy! Jonathan is safe!' Mina cried. 'He has been very ill. But now he is asking for me. I do not want to leave you. You are not well. But I must go to Budapest.'

'Of course, my dear,' Lucy said. 'You must go to Budapest.'

Mina travelled by train to Budapest. It was a long journey. At last, she was able to hold her dear Jonathan in her arms. How thin and pale he was! 'Why didn't you tell me you were ill?' Mina asked. 'What happened at Castle Dracula?'

'I cannot talk about Castle Dracula now,' Jonathan whispered. 'Terrible things happened there. Was I ill – or mad? I don't know. I can't tell you about it now. I will tell you all about it later.'

'Jonathan,' Mina said, 'forget what has happened. You must get well. Then we will begin our new life – together.'

'Yes,' Jonathan whispered. 'But we will get married at once. I will never leave you again!'

Mina and Jonathan were married on 1st September in Budapest. They did not reach England until 18th September. The weather in London was fine and warm. Mina and Jonathan drove slowly through the city in the early evening. The streets were full of happy people.

Suddenly Jonathan gave a terrible cry.

'My God, look!' he said. 'It is the Count!'

Jonathan pointed at a tall man who was talking to a beautiful young woman. The man had a cruel, white face. As he smiled, Mina saw his red lips and sharp, white teeth.

'Count Dracula is here in London!' Jonathan cried. 'I was not mad. Those things did happen in Castle Dracula!'

'Please, Jonathan, you will be ill again,' Mina said. 'The Count has a house near London. Why shouldn't he be here?

'There is terrible danger,' Jonathan told her. 'I will tell you all about it when we get home.'

As they drove up to their home, a servant opened the door. She held out a telegram.

'This has just arrived, madam,' she said.

The telegram was from Doctor Arthur West, Lucy's husband. As Mina read it, her eyes filled with tears. The message was very short.

My dear wife is dead. She was buried[28] *yesterday. Arthur.*

'Lucy dead? I can't believe it,' Jonathan said quietly. 'How did it happen?'

'Arthur must come and stay with us,' Mina said. 'I'll send him a telegram at once.'

That night, Jonathan told Mina all about Castle Dracula. He told her the terible things that had happened there. And now Count Dracula was in England. What was he planning to do?

5

How Lucy Died

When Arthur West arrived at the Harkers' home, he was dressed all in black. His face was pale and sad. The three friends had many things to talk about. After dinner, Mina spoke to him quietly.

'Arthur, dear, Lucy's death has been a great shock to us both. Can you tell us how she died?'

'I returned from Amsterdam about a week after you left Hythe,' Arthur replied. 'By that time, Lucy was very ill. Her face was pale and she was very thin. I examined[22] her, but I could not find anything wrong.'

'Was Lucy still leaving her bed at night? Was she still walking in her sleep?' Mina asked.

'Yes,' Arthur said. 'And she began to have strange dreams. She saw red eyes and golden dust moving in the air.'

'Golden dust?' Jonathan repeated slowly. 'Is the Count at work already? Go on, Arthur, I will tell you my story later.'

'The dreams worried me,' Arthur went on. 'I sent a telegram to Professor Van Helsing in Amsterdam. He came to Hythe immediately.

'When Van Helsing arrived, Lucy was too ill to get out of bed,' Arthur told his friends. 'Van Helsing examined her with great care. He told me that Lucy had lost a lot of blood[23]. She needed a blood transfusion[24] to save her life. I told the Professor to take the blood from me.'

'Oh God,' Jonathan said quietly. 'Were there any marks on Lucy's throat – small, red marks?'

Arthur looked very surprised.

'Yes, there were. How did you know?' he said. 'The marks worried the Professor very much.'

'Did the blood help Lucy?' Mina asked.

'Yes, she looked better at once,' Arthur replied. 'And she had a quiet night. In the morning she was well and happy. Van Helsing visited her and brought lots of garlic[25] plants!'

'Then the Professor knew,' Jonathan said quietly.

'Knew what?' Arthur asked. 'The garlic had a very strong smell. But Van Helsing put it all round our bedroom. Then he twisted some of the white flowers together and put them around Lucy's neck.'

'Why didn't the garlic keep Lucy safe?' Jonathan said. 'I cannot understand it.'

Arthur told his friends the rest of the story. Van Helsing stayed in Hythe for a few days. Slowly, Lucy grew stronger.

One night, Arthur went out to visit a sick child. Van Helsing was in the library reading. Lucy was sleeping in her room. The garlic flowers were round her neck and she looked very beautiful. The bedroom window was shut.

'I was away for several hours,' Arthur went on. 'It was morning when I returned, but the house was silent. I went into the library. Van Helsing was sleeping in the chair. I called his name but he did not wake. Suddenly I was afraid. I ran upstairs and into our bedroom. The window was broken. There was glass all over the floor! Lucy lay on the bed with her eyes closed. She had pulled the garlic flowers away from her neck.'

Arthur stopped talking. There were tears in his eyes. After a few moments, he went on.

'I ran to get Van Helsing,' Arthur said. 'I called his name many times before he woke. Then he hurried with me to Lucy's bedroom. When Van Helsing saw Lucy, he told me she was dying. The marks on her throat had gone. Van Helsing said we must wake Lucy immediately. She must not die in her sleep.

'At that moment, Lucy opened her eyes. She looked at me and smiled. Then she spoke to me. Her voice was slow and strange. She told me a man had come to the window. He had called her again and again. She had opened the window and asked the man to come in.

'Lucy took hold of my hand. Her fingers were as cold as ice. Lucy asked me to kiss her. But as I leant over, Van Helsing pulled me away. Then Lucy's face became angry. Her eyes were cruel, she was ugly, I . . .'

Arthur covered his face with his hands. 'It was terrible,' he said. 'She did not look like Lucy at all.'

'Poor Lucy,' Mina said and she held Arthur's hand. 'Did the poor girl die peacefully[26]?'

'Yes, thank God,' Arthur replied. 'When she opened her eyes, she was beautiful again. But Van Helsing would not let me kiss her lips. So I kissed her hand and her long black hair. Then she died. Dear Lucy is at peace now.'

'Is she at peace?' Jonathan said slowly. 'Has the Professor gone back to Amsterdam?'

'Yes, he has,' Arthur replied. 'But he said he would return if

'Dear Lucy is at peace now.'

anything happened to Lucy. I did not understand him. Lucy is dead.'

Mina looked at her husband. Their eyes were full of fear. Had Dracula been drinking Lucy's blood? Was she a vampire too?

6

The Beautiful Lady of Hythe

After a few days, Arthur West returned to his lonely house in Hythe. Jonathan and Mina did not say anything to Arthur about their fears. But they read the newspaper carefully every day. Then one morning, Jonathan saw these words.

THE BEAUTIFUL LADY OF HYTHE

The young mothers of Hythe are very afraid. Something very strange is happening in this little town by the sea. Some young children have disappeared from their homes. When they were found, the children were safe. But they all told the same strange story. They had met a beautiful lady with long black hair. She had smiled at them and kissed them. All the children were found again in the old churchyard on the hill. They were very pale and they all had small, red marks on their throats. Who had taken them there? Was it the beautiful lady? What had made the marks on the children's necks? There have been no answers to these questions.

'Is Lucy the beautiful lady?' Mina asked. 'Are the little children her first victims[27]?'

'I'm afraid they are,' Jonathan answered. 'I will send a telegram to Van Helsing at once. He is the only man who can help us – and poor Lucy too.'

Professor Van Helsing left Amsterdam as soon as he received the telegram. He went at once to the Harkers' home in London.

Mina welcomed the old man with tears in her eyes.

'Thank you for coming so quickly,' she said.

'We do not have much time,' Van Helsing answered. 'I will do all I can to help.'

That night, Jonathan told the Professor about Castle Dracula. The Professor asked many questions.

'You were lucky to get away from Castle Dracula,' the Professor said at last. 'Vampires have terrible powers. Count Dracula is the most powerful of them all!'

'And I helped him to come to England,' Jonathan whispered. 'What does he plan to do here? Can we stop him?'

'Let me tell you all I know about vampires,' Van Helsing answered. 'I have studied their history and read many books about them. Some vampires are hundreds of years old. They live on blood, which they take from living people. But vampires stay alive after they have been buried. Their victims die when they have lost all their blood. Then they become vampires too!'

'That is what happened to poor Lucy,' Mina said sadly. 'How can we help her. Is there anything we can do?'

'We have to do three things to stop the vampire,' Van Helsing replied. 'First we must open Lucy's coffin[29]. Then we must hammer a sharp piece of wood through her heart. Lastly her head must be cut off. Then she can rest forever.'

'Dear Lucy, how terrible,' Mina said quietly. 'How can we tell poor Arthur?'

'We must go to Hythe at once, Mina,' the old Professor said. 'We must help Lucy as quickly as we can. We all loved her. We are the only ones who can help her.'

'I shall be happy to help,' Jonathan said quietly.

'After we have helped Lucy, we must fight the Count himself,' the Professor said. 'No one in England is safe until the greatest Vampire of all is destroyed!'

The three friends left immediately for Hythe. They told Arthur that Lucy had become a vampire. At first he was very angry. But Jonathan told Arthur what had happened at Castle

Dracula. Then Arthur knew that their terrible story was true.

Arthur, Jonathan and Van Helsing went to the churchyard late that night. Lucy West had been buried in the family vault[30] in the churchyard. The Professor was carrying a large bag. Arthur opened the vault with his key. The three men stood quietly round Lucy's coffin.

'Look carefully,' the Professor said. 'The vault has not been opened since Lucy's funeral, has it? Now, watch!'

Then, with a long piece of iron, Van Helsing began to open Lucy's coffin.

'There,' he said as he lifted the lid.

At first, Arthur did not want to look. Lucy had been dead for nearly two weeks. Then he gave a terrible cry.

'My God! The coffin is empty!' he shouted. 'Where is my wife?'

'I can answer that,' Jonathan said quietly. 'Lucy needs blood. She is looking for another victim!'

'It is true,' Van Helsing said. 'Let us wait in the churchyard for Lucy to come back.'

They left the vault and Arthur locked it again. Van Helsing led them to a dark part of the churchyard. They waited. The time passed very slowly.

Then, in the moonlight, they saw something white move towards Lucy's vault. Arthur gave a cry and stepped forward.

'My God, it is Lucy!' he shouted.

The thing turned its head and looked straight at them. The moon was very bright and the three friends could see everything clearly. What they saw filled them with fear.

Yes, it was Lucy. Her face and long, dark hair looked the same. But the eyes shone with a terrible red light. Blood was running from her red lips onto her white dress. She smiled and they could see her sharp, white teeth.

'Arthur, my love, come to me,' she whispered. She held out her hands and walked towards him. 'Come to me now, and never, never leave me.'

Arthur took another step forward. Lucy opened out her arms to hold him. Van Helsing ran in front of Arthur and held up a large cross.

When Lucy saw the cross, she stopped smiling. Her face became cruel and angry. She made a noise like an animal and ran towards the vault. It was shut and locked, but the vampire disappeared inside.

'Oh, God! Was that terrible thing my Lucy?' Arthur cried.

'That is not the dear woman you loved,' Van Helsing told him. 'It is the vampire that is using her body. But if we are strong, we can help Lucy to rest peacefully. Give me my bag, Jonathan.'

They entered the vault again. It was almost dawn. When Van Helsing opened the coffin, they saw the vampire. Her eyes were open and she smiled at them. It was a terrible smile.

Van Helsing opened his bag. He took out a long, sharp stake[31] and a hammer. Then he looked at Arthur.

'I shall hold the stake and point it at her heart,' the Professor said. 'Then, as we pray, hammer it down.'

With a last look at the thing in the coffin, Arthur raised the hammer. He brought it down – once, twice, many times. Terrible screams came from the vampire's blood-covered lips. The white dress became red as the stake went into Lucy's body.

They all prayed. At last, the thing in the coffin stopped moving. Arthur dropped the hammer and almost fainted.

'Look,' Van Helsing said, 'now she is at peace.'

There, in the coffin, lay Lucy. She was dead and at peace. All the blood had gone and there was a beautiful smile on her face.

'Now you can kiss your wife,' Van Helsing said. Arthur kissed Lucy once on the lips. Then he turned and left the vault.

Van Helsing and Jonathan worked together. They cut off Lucy's head. Then they closed the coffin lid and hammered it down.

When they left the vault, it was daylight. Birds were singing and the air was warm.

'We have begun our work,' Van Helsing said to Jonathan and Arthur, 'but we have not finished it. Now we must find Count Dracula. We must destroy him forever!'

7

The House of the Vampire

After they had left the vault, the friends slept for several hours. Then later in the day, they met to make their plans.

'We are all in danger,' Van Helsing said. 'Dracula must know that he has enemies in England. He will soon find out what we are doing. Then he will attack us.'

'Why don't we attack him first?' Arthur cried. 'We must go to his house together. Where is his house, Jonathan?'

'I can't remember,' Jonathan replied slowly. 'It's very strange. I think Dracula has made me forget. All the papers about his house are in my office in London.'

'Then let us all go back to London quickly,' said Van Helsing. 'We must find out where Dracula is hiding. It will be safer if we are all together. The Vampire is very powerful.'

They went to London and Jonathan hurried to his office. But he could not find the papers. They had all been taken. He returned home at once. He told the others what had happened.

'Dracula has taken the papers,' Van Helsing said. 'He knows he is in danger. He knows we are his enemies. But vampires have no power during daylight. In daylight, Dracula rests in one of the boxes from Transylvania. They must be in his house.'

'But where is his house?' Mina cried.

The old Professor thought for a moment. Then he looked at Jonathan carefully.

'If you agree, I shall hypnotise[32] you,' he said. 'Then you may remember where Dracula's house is.'

'Yes, I agree,' Jonathan said. 'Do what you can, Professor. I am ready.'

Van Helsing sat opposite Jonathan and spoke to him quietly. The young man's eyes closed. He began to breathe more slowly.

'Count Dracula has a house near London. Where is it, Jonathan?' the Professor asked. Jonathan answered in a slow, clear voice.

'The Count is living to the east of London,' he said. 'His house is very big and very old. There is a high wall round it.'

'How did you get there, Jonathan?' asked Van Helsing.

'The nearest railway station is about a mile away from the house . . .'

'What is the name of the station, Jonathan?' Van Helsing asked.

'It is difficult to remember. There is a mist in front of my eyes. Now the mist is going. The name is . . . Purfleet. The . . . the mist is coming back, a golden mist. I can see red eyes . . . they are looking for me . . .'

'Wake up, Jonathan!' the Professor said quickly. Jonathan opened his eyes.

'You were in danger,' Van Helsing said. 'Dracula knew what I was doing. We do not have much time.'

'What shall we do?' Arthur asked.

'We must get into Dracula's house and look for the boxes of earth,' Van Helsing replied. 'You must stay here, Mina. Don't leave the house. Dracula is not far away. Remember what happened to Lucy.'

'We cannot leave Mina here on her own!' Jonathan cried.

'She will be safe,' the Professor said. 'No vampire can enter a house unless he is invited in. Lucy walked in her sleep and Dracula met her in the churchyard. Stay in the house, Mina, and you will be safe.'

The three men left the Harkers' house in the afternoon. The things they needed were in their bags. They went by train. When they reached Purfleet station, the Professor asked a few questions. A man at the station was able to answer them.

A tall, dark stranger had bought a big house not far from the station. Later, fifty huge boxes had been sent to the house. The stranger was living there alone.

The three friends were sure that the stranger was Dracula. Very soon they were on the road to the house. As they walked, they became more and more tired.

At last, they reached the old house. But the daylight had almost gone. Van Helsing looked at his friends.

'It is dark. We are late,' he said. 'Dracula will have left the house. While he is away, we will destroy his resting places.'

The high wall of the garden was broken in one place. They were able to climb it easily. The garden was silent and empty. The house was dark. At the back of the house, they found a broken window. They were soon inside.

The old house was full of dust. The air smelt unpleasant and it was very cold. Every room was empty. Then at the end of a long passage, they found a large wooden door. The key was in the lock and Van Helsing turned it slowly. There was a terrible smell that reminded Jonathan of Castle Dracula.

'This place smells of blood,' Arthur West whispered. As he held up his lamp, rats ran away from the light. Some steps went down to the old chapel. There on the cold, wet stones were the wooden boxes.

'Those are the boxes I saw in Castle Dracula,' Jonathan said quietly.

'We must work quickly,' the Professor said, opening his bag. 'Dracula must not find us here. Inside every box we will place some holy bread[33]. Then the Vampire will be in our power.'

The men worked for many hours. One by one, the boxes were opened. Then holy bread was placed on the earth inside. The lids were hammered down. The two young men worked together. Old Van Helsing stood by the open door at the top of the steps. He held a cross in his hand. Jonathan and Arthur had one more box to open. Suddenly Van Helsing gave a cry.

'The Count! The Count!' he shouted down to them. 'The Vampire is coming back. We have no more time. Leave the last box and follow me!'

One box was left unopened. Jonathan and Arthur ran up the stone steps and after the Professor. As they reached the broken window, they heard a terrible cry. They turned quickly. Count Dracula was coming towards them. His face was white and angry. His eyes shone with red fire.

When the Vampire saw Jonathan, he jumped at him like a wild animal. But Van Helsing stood in front of Jonathan and held up his cross. Dracula stepped back.

'You cannot stop me,' he cried out, 'I am Dracula! I have lived and fought my enemies for hundreds of years. I have fought armies. How can three men stop me now?'

Suddenly the house was full of strange mist. The three friends got out of the window and ran across the garden. They found the broken part of the wall and climbed over.

In the road, the air was clear. The moonlight shone on the men's white faces.

'Come,' said Van Helsing, 'we must get back to Mina. She may be in danger.'

The three friends hurried to the little station. They caught a train to London.

When they reached Jonathan's house, it was quiet. Jonathan unlocked the front door and the three men went upstairs to their own bedrooms.

Jonathan opened his door quietly and then he gave a terrible cry. His friends ran into the room after him.

The bedroom window was wide open and moonlight was shining into the room. Mina was on the balcony[34] and a dark shape was leaning over her. It was Count Dracula!

One of his hands held the back of Mina's neck. The other held down her hands. But the Vampire was not drinking Mina's blood. No, it was more terrible than that. Dracula was holding

Mina's face to a long cut on his chest. He was making her drink his blood!

The Vampire turned his head. His eyes burned with a terrible red light. Blood was dripping from his red lips and long, white teeth. The Vampire had already taken his meal of blood!

Dracula gave a cry of anger, but Van Helsing was ready for him. The old doctor held his cross up high. A cloud covered the moon. It was suddenly dark. When the moonlight shone again, Dracula had gone. A little golden dust moved over the balcony.

Poor Mina was almost mad with fear. When she saw Jonathan, she began to cry and cry. Van Helsing carried Mina back to the bed. Then he washed the blood from her face and neck.

'My dear Mina,' the old man said. 'You are safe now. Can you tell us what happened?'

'Oh, Jonathan, why did you leave me?' Mina cried.

'I thought you were safe,' Jonathan answered as he held his wife's hands.

'I was asleep,' Mina said. 'I was dreaming. I saw a cloud of golden dust. I saw eyes burning with red fire. Something woke me. It was the sound of a child, crying. When I got up, I saw something moving in the garden. I opened the window and walked out onto the balcony. Then suddenly, he was standing beside me. I saw his red eyes, his cruel mouth and his long, white teeth. I knew it was Count Dracula! He smiled and said, "Nothing can help you now. You are in my power . . ." '

Mina covered her face with her hands.

'Then he put his lips to my throat and drank my blood,' she whispered. 'I could not stop him. And now I have drunk his blood. I am a vampire too!'

'No, no!' Jonathan cried.

'It is the truth,' Mina replied. 'I have drunk the Count's blood and I am in his power. I must do what he wants, even if I harm[35] you, my husband!' Then Mina looked at Van Helsing with tears in her eyes.

'The Vampire has won,' she said.

'No!' Van Helsing cried. 'He is afraid, I am sure of it. He cannot stay in England now. He will use the last box to return to his own country. Sleep now, Mina. You must rest.'

But Mina went on speaking.

'I have drunk the Count's blood and I am in his power,' she said. 'But perhaps we can use this power to destroy him. Hypnotise me, Professor, before dawn. I think I can tell you what the Vampire plans to do.'

Van Helsing sat down beside Mina and moved his hand before her face. Her eyes closed.

'Where is Count Dracula? What does he plan to do?' Van Helsing asked.

'It is dark,' Mina replied. Her voice was slow and clear. 'I can hear moving water. Oh, the Vampire's power is strong. But I hear a ship and men shouting. The ship is ready to leave. There is a mist, darkness . . . I cannot tell you any more . . .'

In a few minutes, Mina had opened her eyes.

'We have won!' Jonathan told her. 'The Vampire is leaving England. We are safe now.'

But Professor Van Helsing shook his head sadly.

'Have you forgotten? Mina has drunk the Vampire's blood – he has drunk hers. If Mina dies before Dracula is destroyed, she will be a vampire forever!'

8

The Flight of the Vampire

Count Dracula's plan had failed. The Vampire was returning to his own country. In Transylvania he would be safe. If the Vampire reached Castle Dracula he could rest and grow strong again. And while he lived, Mina was in terrible danger. Count Dracula had to be destroyed before he reached his castle.

Arthur and Jonathan went to the Port of London[36] the next day. They found that a ship called the *Queen Catherine* had left for Varna. Varna was a port on the Black Sea. Dracula had travelled from Varna in July!

When it was dark, a tall man had carried a huge wooden box onto the *Queen Catherine*. The man was Count Dracula! A thick mist had covered the ship before it sailed. And Dracula was in the box.

The three men began to make their plans at once. Mina was resting in her room.

'Vampires cannot cross water without help,' the Professor

explained. 'But Dracula is travelling by ship because it is easier. He will not have to move his box until the ship reaches land. When the ship reaches Varna, Dracula will wait for darkness. Then he will carry the box from the ship. Later, the box, with the Count inside, will be taken to Castle Dracula. There, the Vampire will be safe.'

'Then we must follow him!' Arthur cried. 'We must . . .'

Van Helsing held up his hand. 'Before we decide what to do,' he said, 'I have something to tell you. Mina must not know our plans.'

'Why not?' Jonathan cried angrily. 'Dracula has harmed her most of all.'

'But the Vampire has power over Mina,' the Professor replied. 'Perhaps he knows what she is thinking. Anything we tell her – he will know.'

No one spoke. Van Helsing and Arthur looked at their friend sadly.

'You are right.' Jonathan said at last. 'I will not tell Mina anything.'

'Then let us follow Dracula,' Arthur said. 'I have money. We could hire a small, fast ship and . . .'

'No, we must follow Dracula by land,' Van Helsing replied. 'He will make the ship go quickly. But the ship will take two weeks to reach Varna. By land, we can get there in a few days.'

'So we shall be waiting for him when he reaches Varna,' Jonathan said.

'No, not you, Jonathan,' Van Helsing said. 'You must stay here and look after Mina.'

As he spoke, the door opened. Mina stood there. Her face was pale.

'No one will stay here to look after me,' she said. 'I am going with you.'

'You will be in great danger if you come with us,' the Professor said. 'The nearer you are to Dracula . . .'

'I know the danger, Professor,' Mina replied. 'If Dracula calls me to him, I shall have to go. But you can hypnotise me. Then I can tell you where the Count is.'

The Professor smiled.

'You are right, dear Mina,' he said.

Mina held Jonathan's hand and looked at her friends.

'Every day, Dracula has more power over me,' Mina said. 'If his power becomes too strong, you must kill me.'

At last, the three men agreed.

'Thank you,' Mina said quietly. 'Remember, if I become a vampire, I shall be your enemy, too!'

In the second week of October, the four friends began their journey across Europe. They took the fastest trains and, in a few days, they were in Varna.

Professor Van Helsing hypnotised Mina every day. He hypnotised her before dawn and before darkness came. Dracula's power was not as strong then. Mina always said the same words.

'Everything is dark. I can hear the wind. I hear the sound of moving water.'

So the friends knew that Dracula had not left the ship. They stayed in Varna waiting for news. More than a week passed. Every day, Arthur went to the port. He asked if the *Queen Catherine* had arrived. Then at last news came.

When Arthur told the others, his face was white.

'The *Queen Catherine* arrived at Galatz, at one o'clock today,' he said.

'My God! What shall we do?' Jonathan cried. 'Where is Galatz?'

Mina looked at her map.

'Galatz is a port on the River Danube,' she said. 'It is more than 200 kilometres away.'

'We must get a ship,' Arthur said. But Jonathan did not agree.

'I think we should go by train,' he said.

'What will Dracula do?' Mina asked slowly. 'Will he go to Castle Dracula by water or by land? It is nearly sunset,' she went on. 'Professor, hypnotise me. I shall tell you what I can.'

Van Helsing did as Mina asked. At first she could not answer his questions. But at last she spoke.

'I hear the sound of water. The water is moving fast. I hear birds singing. It is dark, dark . . . I cannot tell you any more. His power is too strong.'

9

The Return to Castle Dracula

The friends took two days to reach Galatz. They were nearer to Dracula now. Mina was pale and ill. Sometimes she could not answer Van Helsing's questions. The Professor took Mina to a hotel to rest. Arthur and Jonathan tried to get news of Dracula.

They soon returned. Dracula's box was on a fast boat. The Vampire was travelling up the River Seruth.

The River Seruth went high up into the Carpathian Mountains. Castle Dracula was 20 kilometres from the river.

'We must stop Dracula before he reaches the castle.' Van Helsing told them. 'In his tomb, the Vampire will be safe. And then Mina will be in his power forever.'

'We must go up the river after him,' Jonathan said quickly.

'You and Arthur must do that,' the Professor replied. 'Mina and I will go by land to Castle Dracula. We will get there before the Vampire. I will put holy bread in Dracula's tomb.'

On 23rd October, Mina and Van Helsing went by train to Veresti. At Veresti, the Professor bought a small carriage and four fast horses.

It was winter and it was very cold. Wolves were near and they howled day and night. Professor Van Helsing hypnotised Mina every day. She always said the same words.

'It is dark. It is dark. I can hear fast-moving water.'

Mina slept all day and Van Helsing could not wake her. But as soon as night came, she woke up. The Professor was afraid. Mina was pale and thin. Her face was changing. She was becoming more and more like a vampire. Would Mina die before Dracula could be destroyed?

When they crossed the high mountains, snow was falling. At Bistritz, Van Helsing bought new horses. They reached the Borgo Pass early in the afternoon.

On the right, was the narrow road to Castle Dracula. The tall mountains were covered with snow. The strong wind moved the snow in the air. The howling wolves were closer now. Had Dracula sent them?

The old Professor was not afraid. He drove up the narrow road until it was dark. That night, Mina was very excited. Her eyes shone brightly but she would not eat. Every day Dracula's power was stronger.

The Professor had made a fire. He took some of the holy bread and broke it into pieces. Then he placed the pieces in a circle on the ground around Mina.

Mina was watching Van Helsing carefully. She did not move. Her face went white.

'Come closer to the fire,' the Professor said. Mina stood up, walked a few steps and stopped. She could not move out of the circle. Van Helsing covered Mina and himself with thick cloaks. Wolves howled. But Mina and Van Helsing were safe inside the circle.

The snow went on falling. It moved round and round in the wind. And then there was mist and snow.

As the mist moved in the wind, it changed into three beautiful women. They were the three vampires that Jonathan had seen in Castle Dracula!

The vampires laughed and called to Mina from outside the circle.

'Come, sister, come!' they cried. 'You are like us now.'

But Mina turned away and the vampires could not enter the circle.

They called to Mina all night. But when the dawn came, the beautiful women changed back into mist. Mina slept.

In the morning, the four horses were dead. Van Helsing made the fire as big as he could. He left Mina sleeping inside the circle. Then the old Professor started to walk up the narrow road to Castle Dracula.

The snow was very deep and the wind blew into the Professor's face. His bag was heavy. He was cold and afraid. He felt the Vampire's power around him.

Castle Dracula looked black against the white mountains. Van Helsing went on.

At last, he reached the terrible building. When he came to the chapel door it was wide open! But the air inside smelt terrible and he could not breathe.

The chapel was full of old tombs. One tomb was bigger than the others. On it was written the name "DRACULA".

When Van Helsing opened the tomb, he saw it was empty. The Professor opened his bag. He took out some holy bread. He put the bread inside the tomb and closed the lid. The Vampire would never enter it again.

Then Van Helsing found the tombs of the three women vampires. They looked very beautiful. Their eyes were open and they smiled at him. The old Professor looked at them for a moment. But then he remembered Lucy.

As the mist moved in the wind, it changed into three beautiful women.

He took sharp stakes and hammered them through the vampires' hearts. How they screamed as he hammered down the stakes! But when the Professor cut off their heads the vampires changed. There was nothing in the tombs but dust!

Then Van Helsing left that terrible place. Slowly he walked down the road to Mina.

'My husband is near,' Mina called out. 'Quickly, I must go to Jonathan.'

The snow had stopped falling. The air was clear and cold. It was almost sunset and the sun was red in the sky. To the north, Castle Dracula was a great, black shape on the side of the mountain. Far below them, the River Seruth was black against the snow.

They could see a narrow, winding road which went up the side of the mountain. Along this road, a cart[37] was moving quickly. On the cart was a huge wooden box. Dracula was returning to his castle! Professor Van Helsing put his arm around Mina, but she was not afraid.

'Look,' she whispered.

Behind the cart were two men on horses. 'It is Jonathan and Arthur!' Mina cried. 'And they are moving faster than the cart!'

'The sun is going down behind the mountains,' Van Helsing said. 'Dracula must be destroyed before the light has gone.'

Jonathan and Arthur were galloping faster and faster. Their shadows were long and black on the snow. At last, the two friends reached the cart.

The driver tried to hit Arthur but Jonathan pulled the man down from the cart. They fought together for a moment and then the man ran off, shouting with fear.

The black shadows had grown longer now. The light had almost gone. Was there time to destroy the Vampire?

Jonathan jumped onto the cart. He pushed the huge wooden box down onto the snow. The box broke open.

They could see a narrow, winding road which went up the side of the mountain.

There lay Count Dracula. The last light of the sun shone onto the Count's cruel face. Jonathan's long, sharp stake was above Dracula's heart. As the stake went through the Vampire's body, Dracula gave a terrible cry. Then Arthur's knife cut through the Vampire's throat. There was silence. But there was no blood on the snow. Count Dracula's body was a heap of dust!

Mina ran down the road and Jonathan took his dear wife in his arms. The Vampire was dead. The years of blood and fear were over.

Points for Understanding

1

1 In 1875, Jonathan Harker received a letter from Count Dracula.
   (a) What country was the letter from?
   (b) What did Count Dracula want?
   (c) Why did Count Dracula ask Jonathan Harker to visit him?
2 Jonathan asked the innkeeper at Bistritz to tell him about Count Dracula.
   (a) What did the innkeeper do?
   (b) What did the people at the inn do at first?
3 Jonathan looked up a word in his dictionary.
   (a) Who was saying the word?
   (b) What was the word in English?
   (c) What did Jonathan read in the book Mina had given him?
4 When Jonathan got into the coach, the innkeeper ran up to the window.
   (a) What did the innkeeper say to Jonathan?
   (b) What did the innkeeper give Jonathan?
5 What terrible sound did Jonathan hear when it got dark?

2

1 Count Dracula met Jonathan at the door of his castle.
   (a) What did Count Dracula look like?
   (b) What did his hand feel like?
2 'Can you hear the children of the night?' the Count said to Jonathan. 'Listen to their music.'
   (a) What were the children of the night?
   (b) What was their music?
3 Jonathan noticed two strange things about Dracula.
   (a) What did Jonathan notice about Dracula's teeth?
   (b) What did Jonathan notice about the nails on Dracula's fingers?
4 In the morning, Jonathan was shaving in front of his small mirror.
   (a) Why was Jonathan surprised when he heard Dracula's voice behind him?

(b) What happened when Dracula touched the cross around Jonathan's neck?
(c) What did Dracula do with the mirror?

5 Why did Jonathan begin to think that he was a prisoner in Castle Dracula?

3

1 Jonathan fell asleep in an unlocked room. When he woke up, the air was full of golden dust.
(a) What did the golden dust change into?
(b) What did Dracula do when he came into the room?
(c) What did he say?

2 Dracula asked Jonathan to write three letters to Mina.
(a) Did Jonathan write what he wanted in the letters?
(b) What did Jonathan think that the Count was planning to do?
(c) What was the date Jonathan put on the last letter?

3 On 29th June, Dracula spoke to Jonathan.
(a) What did Dracula say?
(b) What did Jonathan decide to do?
(c) What did Jonathan see from the window in the passage?

4 Jonathan found a way into an old chapel.
(a) How many wooden boxes were in the chapel?
(b) Who did Jonathan find in one of the boxes?
(c) What did he look like?

5 Jonathan heard some men coming. He left the chapel quickly.
(a) What were the men doing to the boxes?
(b) Where was Dracula going?

6 What did Jonathan do?

4

1 Mina received letters from Jonathan. Why was she very worried?

2 Mina went to stay with her friend Lucy West.
(a) Where did Lucy live?
(b) What did they do every day?
(c) Where did Lucy like going to most of all?

3 There was a storm on the night of 8th August. Lucy's servant said that a ship had been wrecked.
(a) Where had the ship come from?

(b) What did the servant say was strange about the ship?
(c) What happened as soon as the ship touched the shore?

4 The ship was full of big, wooden boxes. What was in the box that broke open?

5 That night, Mina woke up. Lucy was not in the bedroom.
(a) Where did Mina find Lucy?
(b) What did Mina notice on Lucy's throat as she put her to bed?

6 After that night, Lucy became paler and paler.
(a) Why did Mina want to send a telegram to Arthur?
(b) Why would Lucy not let her?
(c) Why did Mina lock the bedroom door?

7 One night, Mina found Lucy leaning out of the bedroom window.
(a) What was sitting beside Lucy?
(b) What did Mina notice about the marks on Lucy's throat?

8 Why did Mina have to leave at once?

9 Mina asked Jonathan about Castle Dracula. What did Jonathan reply?

10 Who did Jonathan see on their first evening in London?

11 A telegram was waiting for Mina when she got home.
(a) Who was the telegram from?
(b) What did the telegram say?

5

1 'Before she died, Lucy began to dream strange dreams,' Arthur told Mina and Jonathan.
(a) What did Lucy see in her dreams?
(b) Why was Jonathan surprised?

2 Why did Lucy need a blood transfusion?

3 What questions did Jonathan ask about Lucy's throat?

4 What plants did Professor Van Helsing bring into Lucy's bedroom?

5 Lucy asked Arthur to kiss her. What did Professor Van Helsing do?

6 When Arthur finished telling them about Lucy's death, Mina and Jonathan's eyes were full of fear. What were they afraid of?

6

1 Mina and Jonathan read a strange story in the newspaper.
(a) What had happened to some young children in Hythe?
(b) Where were the children found?
(c) What was strange about their throats?

2 'We have to do three things to stop the vampire,' said the Professor. What were the three things they had to do?
3 Why did Arthur cry out when he looked in the coffin?
4 'We have begun our work,' said Van Helsing. 'But we have not finished it.'
   (a) How had they begun their work?
   (b) What must they do in order to finish it?

7

1 'All the papers about his house are in my office in London,' said Jonathan.
   (a) Why did Jonathan have to find the papers?
   (b) Was he successful?
2 Why did Van Helsing hypnotise Jonathan?
3 What did the three friends put in the boxes in Dracula's house? Did they put something in every box?
4 Back at Jonathan's house, they found Mina in terrible danger. What was Dracula making her do?
5 'I think I can tell you what the Vampire is planning to do,' Mina told Van Helsing.
   (a) How could Van Helsing find out from Mina what Dracula's plans were?
   (b) What did Mina tell Van Helsing?
6 What would happen to Mina if she died before Dracula was destroyed?

8

1 'You will be in great danger if you come with us,' Van Helsing told Mina.
   (a) Why would she be in great danger?
   (b) How could Mina help the three friends?
   (c) What did Mina make Jonathan and the two others promise to do?
2 Why did Van Helsing hypnotise Mina early in the morning and in the evening?

9

1 'Mina and I will go by land to Castle Dracula,' said Van Helsing. What did Van Helsing plan to do when he got to Castle Dracula?
2 The Professor was afraid. What was happening to Mina on the journey to Castle Dracula?
3 Mina and Van Helsing were safe inside the circle.
   (a) Could Mina get out of the circle?
   (b) What was keeping them safe?
4 Why could Dracula not get back inside his tomb?
5 Why did Jonathan and Arthur have to destroy Dracula before it became dark?
6 How was Dracula finally destroyed?

Glossary

See also the *Introductory Notes* on page 4.

1 ***sign*** (page 6)
you sign a letter or a paper by writing your name on it. Dracula had to sign the papers in order to buy the house.

2 ***coach*** (page 7)
a coach is pulled by horses. People travelled by coach from one town to another. A carriage is smaller than a coach. It is owned and used by one person.

3 ***inn*** (page 7)
a place where people can eat and drink and stay for the night.

4 ***vampire*** (page 8)
see the *Introductory Notes* on page 4.

5 ***cross*** (page 8)
see the *Introductory Notes* on page 4 and the illustration on page 8.

6 ***wolf*** (page 9)
a large, dangerous animal like a dog. At the time of this story, many wolves lived in the forests and mountains of Eastern Europe. The long, loud noise a wolf makes when it is hungry is called *howling*.

7 ***cloak*** (page 9)
a long coat without sleeves, worn by men and women.

8 ***winding*** (page 11)
the passages and stairs in Castle Dracula were long and turned to the left and right many times.

9 ***chapel*** (page 13)
a small building where people can pray.

10 ***tomb*** (page 13)
a stone covering under which people are laid after they die. Tombs usually have the name of the dead person written on them.

11 ***leaning*** (page 14)
Count Dracula was standing with his face near to Jonathan.

12 ***shave*** (page 14)
to remove the hair from the face with a *razor*.

13 ***couch*** (page 16)
a long seat on which you can sit or lie down.

14 ***faint*** (page 17)
Jonathan was so frightened that he was unable to see, hear or speak for several hours.

15 ***dawn*** (page 18)
early in the morning when the light of the sun first appears in the sky.

16 ***hammer*** (page 19)
to hit something again and again. The men were hitting nails into the lids of the boxes to fix them down. A hammer is a tool used for hitting nails into wood.

17 ***churchyard*** (page 20)
the land around a church where dead people are buried. (See Glossary no. 28)

18 ***excited*** (page 20)
the loud noise of the thunder and the bright light of the lightning excited Lucy. The storm frightened her. But at the same time, she wanted to watch it.

19 ***wrecked on the shore*** (page 20)
the wind and the high waves drove the ship out of the water onto the land.

20 ***shawl*** (page 21)
a cloth worn over the head and shoulders by women.

21 ***telegram*** (page 23)
a quick way of sending messages from one place to another.

22 ***examined*** (page 26)
a doctor examines sick people to find out why they are sick.

23 ***lose a lot of blood*** (page 26)
Van Helsing said that Lucy was pale and ill because she did not have enough blood in her body.

24 ***a blood transfusion*** (page 26)
Lucy needed more blood in her body to make her strong again. Van Helsing took blood from Arthur's arm and put it into Lucy.

25 ***garlic*** (page 27)
see *Introductory Notes* on page 4.

26 ***peacefully*** (page 28)
quietly and happily.

27 ***victim*** (page 30)
vampires attack people and drink their blood. These people are the vampires' victims.

28 ***buried*** (page 25)
when a person dies, they are put into the ground or a tomb. (See Glossary no. 10)

29 ***coffin*** (page 31)
a wooden box that a dead person is laid in.

30 ***vault*** (page 32)
a building made of stone where dead people are laid in their coffins. Family vaults are large and hold all the coffins of one family. The doors of vaults are usually made of strong wood or metal and are kept locked.

31 ***stake*** (page 33)
a long piece of wood with a sharpened point.

32 ***hypnotise*** (page 36)
to make someone go to sleep in a special way. When Van Helsing hypnotised Jonathan, he was able to say where Dracula's house was.

33 ***holy bread*** (page 38)
see *Introductory Notes* on page 4.

34 ***balcony*** (page 40)
a place where you can sit or stand outside the window of a house.

35 ***harm someone*** (page 42)
to hurt or kill someone.

36 ***Port of London*** (page 43)
a place in London on the River Thames. Ships sail from the Port of London to many places in the world.

37 ***cart*** (page 50)
a cart is pulled by horses. Carts are used for carrying heavy things.

A SELECTION OF GUIDED READERS AVAILABLE AT

INTERMEDIATE LEVEL

Shane *by Jack Schaefer*
Old Mali and the Boy *by D. R. Sherman*
Bristol Murder *by Philip Prowse*
Tales of Goha *by Leslie Caplan*
The Smuggler *by Piers Plowright*
The Pearl *by John Steinbeck*
Things Fall Apart *by Chinua Achebe*
The Woman Who Disappeared *by Philip Prowse*
The Moon is Down *by John Steinbeck*
A Town Like Alice *by Nevil Shute*
The Queen of Death *by John Milne*
Walkabout *by James Vance Marshall*
Meet Me in Istanbul *by Richard Chisholm*
The Great Gatsby *by F. Scott Fitzgerald*
The Space Invaders *by Geoffrey Matthews*
My Cousin Rachel *by Daphne du Maurier*
I'm the King of the Castle *by Susan Hill*
Dracula *by Bram Stoker*
The Sign of Four *by Sir Arthur Conan Doyle*
The Speckled Band and Other Stories *by Sir Arthur Conan Doyle*
The Eye of the Tiger *by Wilbur Smith*
The Queen of Spades and Other Stories *by Aleksandr Pushkin*
The Diamond Hunters *by Wilbur Smith*
When Rain Clouds Gather *by Bessie Head*
Banker *by Dick Francis*
No Longer at Ease *by Chinua Achebe*
The Franchise Affair *by Josephine Tey*
The Case of the Lonely Lady *by John Milne*

For further information on the full selection of Readers at all five levels in the series, please refer to the Heinemann Guided Readers catalogue.

Heinemann International
A division of Heinemann Publishers (Oxford) Ltd
Halley Court, Jordan Hill, Oxford OX2 8EJ

OXFORD LONDON EDINBURGH
MADRID ATHENS BOLOGNA PARIS
MELBOURNE SYDNEY AUCKLAND SINGAPORE TOKYO
IBADAN NAIROBI HARARE GABORONE
PORTSMOUTH (NH)

ISBN 0 435 27220 9

This retold version for Heinemann Guided Readers

First published 1982
Reprinted seven times
This edition published 1992

A recorded version of this story is available on cassette.
ISBN 0 435 27289 6

Illustrated by Kay Dixey
Typography by Adrian Hodgkins
Cover by Ashley Pearce and Threefold Design
Typeset in 11/12.5 pt Goudy
by Joshua Associates Ltd, Oxford
Printed and bound in Malta

93 94 95 96 97 10 9 8 7 6 5 4 3 2